CW00848153

The Tale of
Hilary Hiccup

Jez Alborough

M

MACMILLAN CHILDREN'S BOOKS

When Hilary ate
what a terrible sight!
She hadn't got time
to be prim and polite.
Within a few minutes
a breakfast or dinner
would start at the table
and end up within her.

Her mother would say,
"Can I make a suggestion?
Eating so fast
Could impair your digestion.
Good manners," she told her,
"should always be followed.
Your food should be chewed
before being swallowed."

But Hilary's habit
grew worse every day,
until at one meal
she got carried away.
Her favourite dinner
of spinach and pasta
encouraged Her Highness
to eat even fasta.
She swallowed and gobbled
with never a care –
and down with the food –

went a pocket of air.

It gurgled inside her
and then just as quick
came upwards again
with the sound of a HIC.

HIC went her tummy
and up went her feet,
lifting her skywards
then back to her seat.
"Goodness," thought Hilary,
"What have I done?
With HICcups like this
I could really have fun."

While her poor mother
was quite unaware,
She HICced herself upwards
and out of her chair,
over the table
and on to the floor,
into the hallway
and out through the door.

"Come back!" cried her mum,
as she chased down the garden.
"It's naughty to HICcup
without saying pardon."
But Hilary carried on
into the street,
bouncing as if she had
springs on her feet,

with eyeballs agog
and eardrums a–popping
she quickly improved
on her talent for hopping.
And soon she was able
with consummate ease
to HICcup quite gracefully
over the trees.

A neighbour who saw her
from way down below
was convinced he had witnessed
a small UFO.
"What is it?" he wondered,
restraining his dog.
"It looks like a person
but hops like a frog."

Then Hilary's mother
who still hadn't caught her
ran by in a panic and cried:
"It's my daughter!"
"Woof! woof!" barked the dog
and he started to race,
then suddenly both of them
joined in the chase.

The passengers clapped
when without any fuss,
Hilary HICced herself
over their bus.
(No one had noticed
the sound of a HIC
so they couldn't see how
she had managed the trick.)

To them it looked splendid
to travel by air,
and journey round town
without paying the fare.
To discover the secret
they altered the route
and the driver set off
in a hasty pursuit.

Now after the doctor
was told of this case,
she left all her patients
to join in the chase.
"This condition," she stated,
"is terribly rare
to HIC with such force
that you rise in the air.

It's a case of 'Hicus Upoverus'

I've seen chronic cases
of HICcups before
but none that could lift someone
clean off the floor.
We *must* try to help her,
she's caught on the hop.
The trouble with HICcups
is making them stop."

People came running
from all over town,
each doing their best to get
Hilary down.

"Halt!" cried a policeman,
"Stop hopping around
and try to control
that ridiculous sound.
You're causing unrest
that I cannot ignore:
such antics are strictly
forbidden by law."

When she saw his expression
turn into a frown
Hilary thought she had
better come down.
Now this she could manage
without any strain –
but not without HICcupping
upwards again.

She began to feel wheezy
and queasy and sick,
but the air kept returning
each time with a HIC.
"Help me," she pleaded,
"oh, when will it end?
These HICcups are driving me
right round the bend."

hic!

The sun had gone down,
it was getting quite dark,
when Hilary HICced herself
into the park.
Weeping and wailing
and grasping her tummy
she shouted, "I want to go
back to my mummy.

I wish that I'd listened
and taken more care
not to go swallowing
pockets of air.
Now I feel wheezy
and queasy and sick,
and I cannot get rid of
this horrible HIC."

She grumbled and tumbled,
without even stopping
to see the direction
in which she was hopping.
It was then that she made
quite a lucky mistake
for her HICcupping landed her
down in a lake.

"Help!" screamed her mum,
as the murky brown water
gurgled on top of
the head of her daughter.
But in spite of the shock
of her watery landing
the lake was quite shallow
and soon she was standing.

All of the people
who'd joined in the chase
stood perfectly still
and stared at her face.
Her mother, who'd told her
to eat with more care,
the doctor who'd said,
"This condition is rare,"
the bus load who'd thought
she was saving her money,
the neighbour who'd found it
all ever so funny,

the policeman who'd said she
was breaking the law,
they all held their breath
for a minute or more.

The park was so still
you could hear a watch tick,
as they waited in dread
for the sound of a HIC.
Women were crying
and men stood aghast
as two minutes –
three minutes –
four minutes passed.

Then gradually everyone
shouted and cheered
for never a hint of a HIC
had appeared.

The doctor announced
that she felt quite assured
now Hilary's HICcups were
finally cured.

Hilary's mother ran into the water
and cried with delight
as she cuddled her daughter,
"My sweetie," she murmured
while stroking her hair,
"How did you stop
flying into the air?"

Hilary smiled at her lucky mistake
and explained what occurred
when she fell in the lake –

"I gobbled and swallowed
with never a care
a mouthful of water
without any air.
It was such a surprise
and it happened so quick
that it seems to have stopped
my unstoppable HIC."

When Hilary eats
it's a wonderful sight,
now she's taking the time
to be prim and polite.
With impeccable manners
she nibbles and savours,
discovering textures
and delicate flavours.

But her mother still thinks
she should caution her not
to over-indulge
with the peppering pot.
Though her habits have changed
and her manners are pleasing,
what if she started –

a spasm of sneezing?

First published 1988 by
MACMILLAN CHILDREN'S BOOKS
A division of Macmillan Publishers Limited
London and Basingstoke
Associated companies throughout the world

British Library Cataloguing in Publication Data

Alborough, Jez
    The tale of Hilary Hiccup.
    I. Title
    823'.914[J]   PZ7

        ISBN 0-333-44098-6

    Printed in Hong Kong